Say "No!" to the "N" Word!

Written by:
Dr. Lesley Stephens Hanes

Co Author & Inspiration:
Maia Imani Hanes

Illustrated by: Revo Yanson

Say "No!" to the "N" Word!

This book is dedicated to both of my brilliant daughters Jasmine and Maia, my genius husband Wendell, my dear mother Ophelia, and to my wonderful brother, father, friends, fellow J&J mothers, and numerous community and professional colleagues. Their love and support encouraged me to create this book as a call for the education of all children about this important matter. I am so very grateful for their support and dedication. Special appreciation goes to Maia as the co-creator of this book and to artist Revo for the beautiful illustrations.

Inspiration

In addition, I have been inspired to use my voice to support racial and ethnic equality and to counter hateful language through the works and legacy of such legendary heroes as Maya Angelou, Oprah Winfrey, Michelle and Barack Obama, Deepak Chopra, the Honorable Congressman Elijah Cummings, and many others. I have also been deeply inspired by leaders and those who traveled with my mother, daughters, and myself to Ghana this year, during the 2019 "Jamestown to Jamestown: Year of the Return" journey, led by the NAACP and the Adinkra Group.

Say No to the "n" word

Hello there! Don't use the "n" word.
No, ma'am and no, sirree...
It's not kind and it's not right
for our humanity!

You say it's just a word?
It's more than that, you see—
Look beyond its common use
To its terrible legacy.

The "n" word, and words like it,
are very, very bad –
And there is no good in using it.
None to be had...

It creates poisonous thoughts and encourages dangerous actions to arise...

Even hearing or seeing the "n" word is an awful surprise!

And it makes me very worried about you,
and about me... about our family, friends
and our wonderfully diverse country!

The "n" word is really meant to
make people feel small.
Instead, let's celebrate our gifts
with words that make us stand tall!

This word should not be used to describe anyone at all.
And... no one... yes, no one should use the "n" word, y'all!

Be Golden and Think Positively

Our culture is very, very precious and
our language is too.
Say "NO" to that "n" word --
or it may bite you!

You know that saying the "n" word does not bring us any closer. It's really a fast way for friendships to be over.

Our Music Is Precious

If you didn't already hear, the "n" word
is vile and mean, I say.
So, choose words that bring joy
and happiness today.

You and your words do matter

So remember to use your words carefully
and avoid ones that offend.
Say "NO" to the "n" word, and you'll be
a better person in the end!

CREATORS

Lesley S. Hanes, MD MSc

As a mother and community member, Doctor Lesley's experiences of racism endured by her children, family, friends, community, and herself in multiple settings (including elementary to graduate schools), and hate crimes occurring in her community's high school and beyond, inspired her to write this book. The author believes in the focus of love, light, spirituality, and positive energy for the guidance of all of humanity to a more civilized world, and the appreciation of African diaspora cultures. Professionally, Dr. Lesley has served her community as a pediatric doctor and pediatric emergency medicine specialist, who currently serves as a public health physician.

Dr. Lesley graduated from Brown University in Rhode Island (Class of '98), prior to completing medical school at the University of Pennsylvania (Philadelphia). She performed her pediatric residency and masters program in affiliation with Columbia University (Babies and Children's Hospital and the school of public health, Manhattan) and her fellowship at Jacobi (Bronx).

Dr. Lesley can be followed at the website: www.respectfulwords.com

Maia Hanes

As an elementary school student, Maia excels in multiple facets and is full of sunshine. She likes to sing, act, build robots, cook, sew, make crafts, practice math, Tae Kwon Do, public speaking, and play many sports. In general, she is very social, loves playing outside, and helping others.

Revo Yanson

Is a freelance digital artist and a traditional painter. He earned his bachelors degree in Fine Arts at La Consolacion College School of Arts. He had launched 30 group exhibitions and 5 one-man shows.

A Message to Children, Families, Educators, and Supporters:

This book is written in a simple fashion so that it may be understandable by children and adults. I hope that you use this book to help foster the need for racial and ethnic equality and to end racial hate and xenophobia. As scary as it may be, the truth is that children (even before they are school age), are being indoctrinated to the use of the "N" word and are learning to hate others that is associated with this destructive word. This word has been an acceptable facet in our society, belying our collective failure to effectively rebuke its use and incorporation into our social fabric, educational systems, and beyond.

I believe that the use of the "N" word must to be eradicated and that children need be socialized at an early age that this word is unacceptable to use. I am a true believer at it is never too late to change -- adults who were never taught in a conscious manner or through life lessons not to use this word, should also use this book to reflect upon disregarding the "N" word from their lexicon. As an educational tool, this book can be used to shine light on the problematic use and dangerous history of this word and to foster discussion among individuals, classes, homes, and communities. I hope that you will read this story to your children, allowing them to ask questions and to explore the message's relevance in their lives.

You may wonder why I did not write out the "N" word in this book. I purposely do not spell out this word since many people, from a young age, are socialized to know what the "N" word signifies, its connotation, as well as methods and reasons for use. I do not want this the book itself to become an instrument of hate and oppression, or as a tool to teach racism. Hence, this book should not be banned from any home or institution and should be used in a positive and reaffirming way.

As a call to action, we need to reverse the use of the "N" word and declare that it should no longer be used. We all know that this vile "n" word is used to dehumanize and degrade people, particularly those who are of the African-diaspora, in the effort to maintain the current, global social-economic repressive structure of people. The "N" word is also used towards people who are not immediate members of the African-diaspora, such as people of color, when it is socially and economically opportune for those using the "N" word. At the same time, this word is used to unify those who perceive themselves as more superior and deserving than people of color. Furthermore, no other word should be used in the place of the "n" word to repress, demonize, and dehumanize people. This is vitally important in this day and time, now more than ever — we are living in a culture of hate, where people of the African diaspora are being subjected to violent and harmful acts and xenophobia against immigrants and long-standing residents abound.

I request that you please use this material to foster compassion and pride in standing up against the use of hateful language and the propagation of racist actions where you live and beyond. This book is meant to be universal and translated into multiple languages so that readers around the world may learn that the use of the "N" word is not acceptable. Thank you for reading this book, and I encourage you to share it with many others.

.

This beautiful children's book inspires and encourages us all to Say NO to the "N" Word.

Saying No to the "N" Word is necessary for our children, and all of us, to uphold the principles of equality, integrity, respect, and kindness for all of humanity.

Made in the USA
Middletown, DE
25 May 2024